★ American Girl®

Happy Holidays!

By Lauren Díaz Morgan
Illustrated by Romina Galotta

A GOLDEN BOOK • NEW YORK

© 2021 American Girl. American Girl and associated trademarks are owned by American Girl, LLC.
All rights reserved. Published in the United States by Golden Books, an imprint of Random House Children's Books, a division of
Penguin Random House LLC, 1745 Broadway, New York, NY 10019, and in Canada by Penguin Random House Canada Limited,
Toronto. Golden Books, A Golden Book, A Little Golden Book, the G colophon, and the distinctive gold spine are registered
trademarks of Penguin Random House LLC.

rhcbooks.com
ISBN 978-0-593-38194-6 (trade) – ISBN 978-0-593-38195-3 (ebook)
Printed in the United States of America
10 9 8 7 6 5 4 3 2 1

As the weather turns colder and the days grow shorter, there are lots of holiday celebrations to look forward to! Families have prepared for the holiday season in many different ways: putting up decorations, cooking special meals, making gifts for loved ones, and carrying on family traditions.

For Christmas, Felicity was invited to a ball.
She practiced her dances so she wouldn't step on
anyone's toes! At the ball, she could hardly believe
the fancy feast set out for the guests.

Every year, Kaya looked forward to her tribe's Winter Spirit Dances. She and her family welcomed visitors to the longhouse, where they gathered for a feast.

After the feast, members of the tribe who had received their guardian spirit joined a ceremonial song and dance.

Maryellen loved how her Florida hometown looked in wintertime—stores bright with lights and decorations everywhere—but she always dreamed of seeing snow.

Her wish came true when she visited her grandmom and grandpop, who took her ice-skating for the very first time!

One night in her log cabin on the prairie, Kirsten surprised her family by celebrating St. Lucia Day just like they used to in Sweden. She dressed in a special traditional outfit and brought them a tray of coffee and Christmas bread she had baked with her mama.

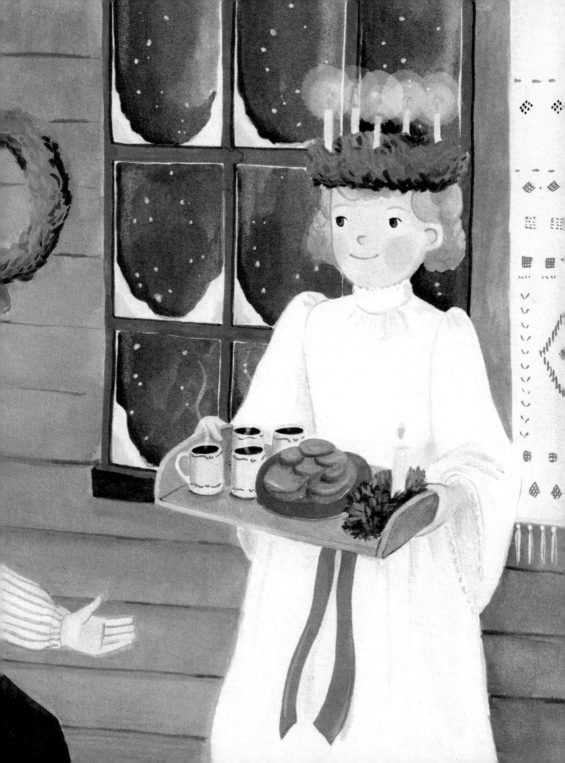

Rebecca's favorite Hanukkah tradition was lighting the menorah. She used the shammash, or helper candle, to light the other candles—one more on each night of Hanukkah.

She also enjoyed playing dreidel with her little brother. The winner was rewarded with candy!

When the first snow of the year came, Molly and her siblings couldn't wait to play outside. They pulled on their snow jackets, boots, hats, and mittens and rushed out to the front yard. It was so much fun that they didn't even mind the cold!

Addy was so excited when Momma showed her how to make her favorite holiday dessert—sweet potato pudding! They shared the yummy treat with friends at a church potluck that night, where they got to watch a shadow play of the Christmas story.

In her village in New Mexico, Josefina played the part of María in Las Posadas, a procession representing María and José's search for an inn on la Noche Buena, or Christmas Eve. Led by her papá, Josefina rode a burro from house to house, singing a special song.

In Hawaii, Nanea and her sister practiced their hula for a holiday performance held by the United Service Organization to cheer up soldiers.

That evening, they sang carols with the whole family,
accompanied by ukulele (and the howls of Mele, their
dog), and wished each other "Mele Kalikimaka," or
merry Christmas.

Julie celebrated Chinese New Year in San Francisco with her best friend, Ivy. They gathered with family to eat Chinese dishes like longlife noodles and bird's-nest soup for good luck. After the delicious meal, Julie and Ivy watched the dragon parade in Chinatown!

Josefina · 1824

Kirsten · 1854

Molly · 1944

There are many different ways to celebrate the holidays, but what they all have in common is spending time together with loved ones—family and friends. What are your favorite holiday traditions?